Naughty Kitty!

ATTENTION!
LOST
WILDE'S SAFARI
DAILY NEWS
WILD ANIMAL LOOSE
There have been several reports by witnesses of a wild creat
seen at large in the local area. It was spotted this morning
"It was NOT spotted," claims Miss Norah Muffin
"It was most definitely striped – like my new curtains."
The local safari park have been informed this m
their new head keeper was not available for com
Residents are advised to stay inside, lock
to explain the recent rash of esca
Chief Fee Line would not
ter is not going

For Mum, who loves cats,
and for Dad, who is allergic – A.S.

A TEMPLAR BOOK

First published in the UK in 2012 by Templar Publishing
This softback edition published in 2013 by Templar Publishing,
an imprint of The Templar Company Limited,
Deepdene Lodge, Deepdene Avenue, Dorking, Surrey, RH5 4AT, UK
www.templarco.co.uk

Copyright © 2012 by Adam Stower

1 3 5 7 9 10 8 6 4 2

ISBN 978-1-84877-331-8

Edited by Libby Hamilton

Printed in China

Naughty Kitty!

by Adam Stower

templar publishing

Lily wanted a doggy,

but her mum said dogs were too messy,

too smelly, and far too much trouble.

So she got Lily something else....

He was a bit scruffy…

and no good at tricks…

but otherwise he
was quite cute,

especially when you
tickled his tummy.

And Mum was right,

he wasn't any trouble at all…

at first.

But then, just for a moment,

NEWS NOW!
MISSING!
Local Safari
park reports
that one of
its animals
is missing!
"A catalogue
of errors led to this cataclysm."
said Theodore Wilder. "This time
not the first time.
it is once more, with feline."

Lily left him alone…

It was a catastrophe.

What a mess!

Lily couldn't understand it.

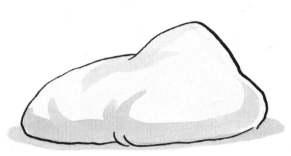

How could you?
Eight fish fingers, all the sticky biscuits,
plums, pickles, Mum's pink party cake,
Dad's Pork chop, the orange pop, two teaspoons
and a washing up sponge!

And she'd just fed him
a whole bowl of Kittibix!

Lily told Kitty to sit still
until she'd finished tidying the kitchen.
There was to be no messing, no mischief
and absolutely no scratching.

Lily was getting cross.

Surely Kitty couldn't cause any more trouble?

But by teatime things had gone from bad to worse.

and I still don't know how
you pinched **all my sausages!**

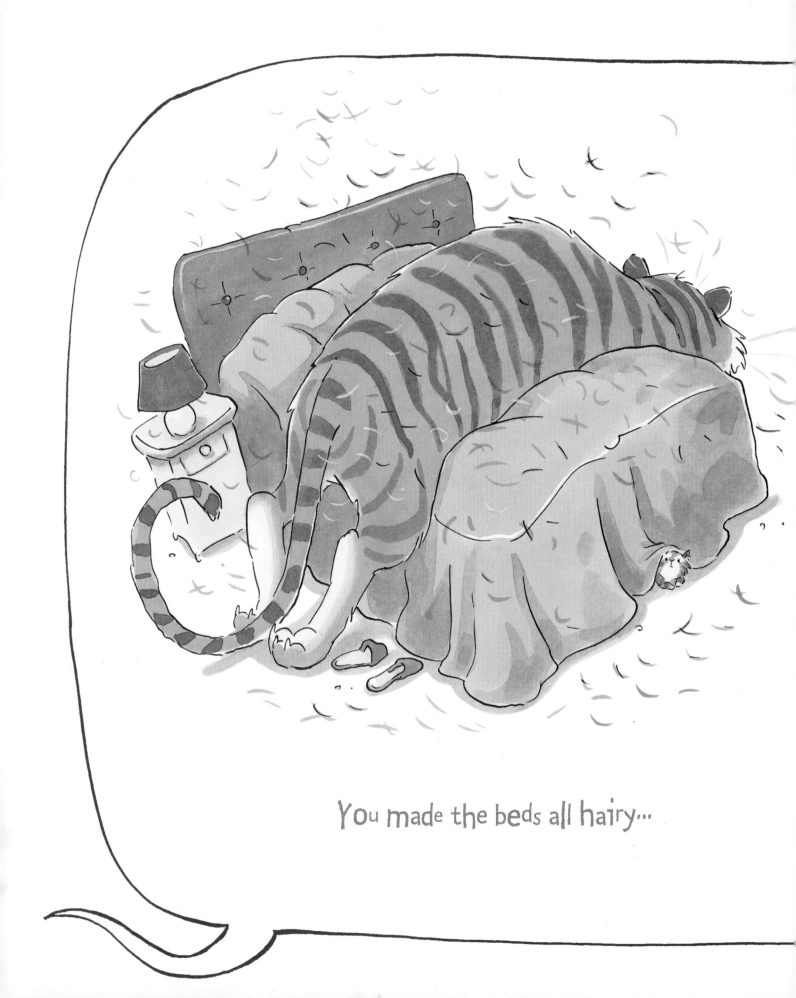

You made the beds all hairy…

and as for Mum's rug –
I can't even talk about that.
It was REVOLTING!

But just then they heard a long, low

GRRRROOOWWWWWWL!

There was something in the garden.

Something with teeth…

something with claws…

something with STRIPES!

It was Pat, the dog from next door.

Lily yelled!

Kitty YOWLED…

...and the bad dog ran away.

Perhaps Kitty wasn't so bad after all.

In fact, Lily decided he was completely fantastic
and he deserved a whole box of Kittibix,
a tummy rub and a quiet, cosy snuggle on the sofa.

So that's just what they did.

AMAZING and TRUE!

FLUFFBUN'S RETURN

Doris Battenburg, 72, of 10 Wye Avenue, Sea Knit, was overjoyed by the recent return of her long lost cat, Fluffbun. "He followed Pat, my dog, home at teatime yesterday. My eyes aren't what they used to but I'm pretty sure it's him. he's grown quite bit since t time I saw him... but at's not surprising, it was 30 years ago."

Doris with Pat and Fluffbun.

MONKEY BUSINESS

It looks like hungry thieves have been targeting poor Mr B. Nana's fruit

Q esp of a l in place

THE HOLE TRUTH

Visitors and staff were baffled this morning when they discovered the local safari park was totally and completely empty.

"Not a sausage! Not even an antelope," claimed new head keeper Bill Loney.

where have all the animals gone?

of UFOs and invisibility rays wer

s are definitely being asked

ecause of

LE in the new park fence, put

e unbas